THE
SIXTY
SECONDS

THE
SIXTY
SECONDS

TED JACKSON

iUniverse, Inc.
Bloomington

The Sixty Seconds

iUniverse books may be ordered through booksellers or by contacting:

iUniverse
1663 Liberty Drive
Bloomington, IN 47403
www.iuniverse.com
1-800-Authors (1-800-288-4677)

Because of the dynamic nature of the Internet, any web addresses or links contained in this book may have changed since publication and may no longer be valid. The views expressed in this work are solely those of the author and do not necessarily reflect the views of the publisher, and the publisher hereby disclaims any responsibility for them.

Any people depicted in stock imagery provided by Thinkstock are models, and such images are being used for illustrative purposes only.
Certain stock imagery © Thinkstock.

ISBN: 978-1-4759-7659-5 (sc)
ISBN: 978-1-4759-7660-1 (ebk)

Printed in the United States of America

iUniverse rev. date: 02/19/2013

Chapter 1

It all started the day Jason feel victim to the juggernaut that corporations were euphemizing as "downsizing." Jason had been employed by the National Integrated System Software Corporation, commonly known as NISS, in Denver for 25 year as a software engineer and fully intended to remain with the same until retirement. He was proud of the job he had done and felt that the company, in turn, had also been loyal to him. In retrospect Jason could now blame only himself for his naivte—if not just plain stupidity. There was no longer any such thing as loyalty—at least on the part of a company. An employee who was loyal was, if not a complete fool, then at least hopelessly short-sighted. The signs of the time were evident for anyone with eyes opened. The problem was that Jason had essentially been keeping his eyes closed—his head in the sand in good ostrich fashion. He had relied simply on the fact that he was doing, and had always done, a good job—putting in many extra unpaid hours to ensure that his work was top notch. It was almost in a state of shock that Jason packed up his personal belongings and hauled them out to his aging BMW. As he pulled down the picture of his wife, Katy, and his two boys, Jeff and Jim, he felt that he had somehow let them down. There were certificates of achievement and excellence and Jason simply threw these in the garbage. Several papers needed to be signed—then Jason turned in his badge and was finished. He walked out the security gate for the last time and wondered what the future held. Some of his colleagues had been updating their resumes and arranging interviews at other software companies but they had had little or no success as there appeared to be a glut of software engineers in the Denver area. Jason had not even bothered to make up a resume—such had been his confidence.

As Jason pulled out of the parking lot onto the busy 50 mph boulevard his thoughts were far removed from his driving. Too late he glanced in the rear view mirror and saw the ten-wheeler bearing down on him at an alarming rate. The vehicle immediately filled the rear view mirror and then there was the sound of screeching brakes. Jason felt the impact of the collision and an instant of searing pain. Then the pain ceased and he found himself back in the line of cars waiting to turn onto the boulevard. He found himself shaking and sweating and a car behind him honked—another angry laid-off engineer wanting to escape the scene. The car in front of him had moved up so Jason inched forward and then pulled up onto the grassy median that separated incoming and outgoing traffic. He then rested his head on the steering wheel and waited for the shaking to subside. He was confused and helpless and needed time to try and figure out what had just happened. He knew that he had been hit by the semi—that much he remembered. How then had he ended up back on the parking lot exit road and not having yet turned onto the boulevard?

His mind refused to function and Jason decided that this was neither the time nor the place to figure things out. He sat in his vehicle for a few minutes and then a polite driver let him get back into the line and he did so. This time he exited with more care and saw the semi roll by that had certainly killed him a minute earlier. Jason needed a drink and a place to sit down and ponder the matter. He passed Smitty's, a local watering hole for NISS employees, but noticed that the parking lot was full. The establishment was certain to be filled with former NISS programmers crying on each other's shoulders. Deciding that this was not what he needed at the time, Jason drove on until he reached a small bar that he had frequented on several occasions. He parked and entered, finding that he was the only customer as the bar had just opened. He replied somewhat shortly to the bartender's "good morning" and ordered a double vokda collins. In the corner stood a cigarette machine and Jason couldn't help himself despite having quit smoking four months earlier. He asked the bartender for change and purchased a pack. He thought about something light but finally reverted to his old standby—Kool Filter Kings. A moment later Jason had a cigarette in one hand and a drink in the other.

He was torn between thinking about the loss of his job and dwelling upon the singular incident with the truck. He decided that he had to understand the truck incident before he could even consider anything else. What exactly had happened? The facts were simple. He had pulled out into the path of an oncoming ten-wheeler and given the driver no chance whatsoever to avoid the collision. The crash had seemed to take place but then conditions had changed to those immediately preceding the turn that had precipitated the collision in the first place. The only explanation that Jason could come up with was that he had somehow imagined the collision—even imagined the concussion of the impact as well as the instant of intense pain. Perhaps the shock of losing his job had something to do with it. Feeling at least semi-satisfied with his conclusion, Jason finished his drink and began to stand up to leave. Suddenly he found himself sitting again with the glass still one third full—the third he had just swallowed or so he had thought. Jason shook his head, finished the drink again and walked out of the bar.

Chapter 2

As Jason drove the 20 miles to his suburban home in Thornton his mind was in a state of turmoil. He knew he would have to find a new job as quickly as possible and that was easier said that done. He was fully aware of the fact that those associates of his who had searched for new jobs had been unsuccessful. A job search now would be even more difficult due to the fact that 100 newly released NISS programmers would now also be in the market. This would simply add to the glut of programmers. Jason wished now that he had trained in some kind of a backup profession such as plumbing or auto mechanics—anything that was at all practical. This was something he had tried to impress upon his sons but to no avail. Jim was enrolled in college at the University of Rochester and majoring in chemical engineering. Jeff was still in high school but showed no interest in attending a trade school for two years before entering college.

Despite the torrent of thoughts in Jason's head, he drove with awareness and care due to the scare he had so recently received. He dreaded facing his wife,

Katy. She was working now but would be home in several hours. She worked at St. Joseph's hospital as a nurse. Jason thought about calling her but decided that the bad news could wait a little longer while he to tried to compose himself somewhat. Also, he would have to apprise Jeff of the news when he got home from school. Jim also needed to be called but that could wait for a few days.

Perhaps the worst problem that Jason faced was the Bricker financial situation. Due to various factors they were quite deeply in debt. One element was the money they had spent on the boys. Since childhood the latter had not lacked for anything—including transformers and GI Joe figures and their various "rides"—whatever the vogue at the time happened to be. They had both attended private schools where tuition, once they reached high school age, rivaled that of many colleges. Jim had initially had a full scholarship to the University of Rochester but, due to some university politics, had lost it. Both boys drove newer cars than Jason and Katy.

At one time NISS had been generous with severance pay but not this time. Jason could count on only 2 months pay as could all of those who had been laid off—regardless of time of service. In times past the policy had been one week of severance pay per year of service which would have given Jason some 6 months to find a job. There had been talk among the laid-off employees that morning of trying to sue the company because of the change of severance pay policy. Jason doubted, however, that anything would come of such a suit as he had never seen anything in print to the effect that the company was obligated to make any severance payments whatsoever. Some of the older employees told him that he was correct and that the company had simply chosen to abide by the one week per service year convention in the past. Now's that it's very survival was threatened, all bets were off.

Finally Jason turned into his driveway and was relieved to note that neither Katy's nor Jeff's vehicles was present. It was hot so he put on a pair of shorts along with a 9th Infantry Vietnam T-shirt. Yes, he had fought for his country but that didn't matter now. The next thing he did was to mix a vodka collins and sit down to think things out. Under the conditions he would have to exercise caution or Mr. Collins would get the upper hand. Jason had already been through periods where drinking had taken over much of his life. He also lit a Kool although he intended to quit smoking shortly—but then again . . . .

The next thing Jason did was to mentally revisit the incident at the plant where he seemed to have been hit by the truck. How could he have so vividly imagined such an occurrence? His only explanation was the one he had come up with at the bar—it must have just been a matter or stress and nothing more. Everyone knew that stress can do strange things to people—it can affect them in many insidious ways. Who knew what effects some of the other now unemployed programmers were suffering. Perhaps his own problem was minor in comparison.

This brought Jason to thinking more about the bar. Was this just a matter of forgetfulness or what? He distinctly remembered finishing his drink and standing up. Then he had suddenly been sitting again with a drink yet to be finished. Once again Jason could only blame the trauma of the entire morning.

Jason soon found himself on his third vodka vollins and decided he'd better do something other than sit and drink. All he needed was for Katy to find him not only jobless but drunk. He decided that his first order of business was to write a current resume—something that he hadn't done for 23 years. He went to his filing cabinet and retrieved a folder labeled "Employment Information." The folder contained little—his original resume and copies of some periodic evaluations by his NISS superiors. He spread these out on his desk, then started up his computer. He already knew how to go about the chore of writing a resume because he had not only observed as his job-searching coworkers had done theirs, but had actually assisted them at times. He was well aware of the fact the new trend in resumes was to get everything on a single page. You were to start with your most recent activity and then work backwards. At every step you were to include what you felt you had done for your company. You were to list your job title, your responsibilities and then how you had fulfilled these responsibilities. Jason did a search of the Internet until he found a resume format that appealed to him. Within an hour and, with the help of Bill Gate's Microsoft Word, he felt that he had a credible document.

With this chore behind him, Jason felt a little better and mixed another vodka collins. He had been in a state of complete concentration and hadn't even thought about the two strange incidents. Next he decided to mow the lawn. He needed something to do to keep from drinking and dwelling on his unemployment. Jason went to the garage and drug out his 15 year old Sears Craftsman mower. As usual it took about 10 tries to get the mower started. Finally the engine caught and he began mowing a swath next to the sidewalk. He was almost to the end of his second swath when it happened. Suddenly he was back in the driveway and attempting to start the mower. The swaths that he had mowed lay untouched.

Jason was shaken. This was the third episode of the day and something strange was indeed happening—something that was unbelievable. It seemed that he was taking little trips back in time. This morning his life had been saved by such a trip. He had indeed been run down by a semi. He estimated that he had gone back about sixty seconds in time on that occasion. The second time around Jason had been able to stop before entering the boulevard and avoid the collision. For that reason and that reason only was he was still alive. The incident at the bar had been a manifestation of the same phenomenon. He had indeed finished his drink the first time. Then came the time irregularity and he was left with a third of his drink untouched. Next came the lawn mower incident.

Jason was frightened but also fascinated as he started the lawn mower again. This time he counted the seconds until he got to where he was had been interrupted the first time. He calculated that his time displacement had entailed a time frame of about 60 seconds. He found himself mouthing "sixty-thousand" as he reached his previous spot in the second swath. This would certainly account for the other two episodes. Apparently anything that happened during that minute was undone after the time had elapsed. It was if nothing had transpired during that time.

Jason now had a million questions and no answers. What was the cause of these time slips or whatever one might choose to call them? Were they and would they always be a matter of 60 seconds in duration? Was he somehow unknowingly invoking the slips? Did he have any control over them? Could he possibly suppress them? Was there any cure at all? Had anyone else suffered something of the sort? Obviously he had far more questions than answers.

Suddenly Jason had another thought. It might be that time was rolling back on its own. It was with all of these thoughts that Jason continued cutting the lawn and he completed the task without further incident. As he pushed the lawn mower toward the garage he heard a car door slam in the driveway and knew that either Jeff or Katy was home. "Hi Dad," said Jeff as he came around the house into the back yard.

"Hi Jeff," responded Jason. "Hold on a minute," he said as he began emptying the lawn mower bag into the garbage can. He the proceeded to tell Jeff about his day—omitting for the time being the time slips. As he was talking Katy pulled in and Jason found himself in tears as he began repeating his report. Katy tried to reassure him but to no avail. She did promise to take over the bill-paying and to help maintain a strict budget. If Jason hadn't found a job within 2 months there would be no alternative for their other son, Jim, except to either get a student loan or to drop out of college. Tomorrow Jason would begin calling the human resources departments of possible employers.

Chapter 3

wo weeks later Jason was totally discouraged. He had, more or less, gone through the yellow pages as far as computers and software companies. The standard message he received was that the concerned company was not hiring at this time but that Jason could call back at a later date if he wished. During the second week he finally got an interview with a small software house. It appeared to Jason, based upon what he was told by the interviewer, that he easily met the qualifications He was then told that he was actually "overqualified." Jason objected quite vehemently and asked how it was possible to be overqualified. The interviewer patiently explained that Jason would undoubtedly "jump jobs" as soon as something became available that was commensurate with his skills. Jason's protests to the contrary got him nowhere. He did get an idea of the direction in which software companies were headed. Wherever possible they wanted to hire new college graduates and then train them, knowing that they would work very cheaply as they usually had no families to support. Finally Jason resorted to a "head hunter" but nothing had happened as the end of two weeks rolled around.

During the two weeks several time slips had occurred but nothing serious happened. While Jason was driving to the store one morning he stopped at a red light. When it changed he proceeded but suddenly found himself back at the same light. With so little knowledge of the phenomenon, Jason had the irrational thought that he might be stuck at the same light forever. But then again the entire thing was irrational. He was indeed living in an irrational world. The slips didn't appear to operate in that manner but who was to say about the future. Jason concentrated upon any type of feeling etc., that might presage an impending attack and believed that he was making some progress. As far as his thoughts they were probably about his current unemployment and the fact that NISS had let him down. Of course NISS was almost always on his mind. However it seemed to Jason that the slips occurred when he concentrated on the letters of the name itself without elaboration. This was followed by a vague sense of unreality—very slight and very transient.

Another episode occurred at Jason's single job interview during that two week period. This one was somewhat embarrassing. When he arrived at the office the secretary was not at her desk. Jason sat down and, when she did appear, he approached her desk and announced his presence. He was told to have a seat and that the interviewer would be right with him. He returned to his chair and suddenly noticed that the secretary was looking at him strangely. Finally she asked him who he was and whom he was there to see. Jason then realized what had happened. The time in which he introduced himself had slipped and he hadn't been aware of it. In the eyes of the secretary she had come out to her desk from the lady's room or wherever and found a man sitting in the office. The man had not approached her but simply remained sitting there. This was rather disturbing but no real harm was done. As far as the interview went Jason was, of course, told that he was overqualified.

There had been several additional episodes but not one else had been involved except for the occasion when Jason and Katy had gone out to eat with Katy's superior and her husband. They had gone to an "all you can eat" Chinese restaurant and Jason had been returning to his table carrying a huge plate of food in one hand and a bowl of soup in the other. He attempted to set the plate on the table but it was unbalanced and he dumped the entire contents in the lap of Katy's boss. He immediately concentrated on the initials "NISS" and was thrilled to find himself back at the food counters. This time he carried the plate in two hands intending to go back for the soup. He was extremely careful and was actually laughing this time when he returned to his table. The other couple asked him what he was laughing about and he could only reply about how funny it would have been it he had dumped the plate on the floor. He added that he was so hungry that he would have had to lap up the food like a dog. The couple laughed indulgently and looked at him rather strangely but said nothing more. As for Jason, he began to realize that there was an upside to these time shifts. First of all one of these had undoubtedly saved his life. Furthermore, depending upon his timing, he could atone for a mistake—actually atone was not the word.

He could actually eliminate a mistake entirely—make it so the mistake never happened.

It was at this point in time that Jason decided that it was time to confide in Katy. He had no idea of how to explain what was going on nor could he realistically expect her to believe him anyway. Not that she would necessarily disbelieve him—she just wouldn't understand nor could he expect her to do so. She would attribute the entire matter to some mental problem and, in fact, he still hadn't entirely ruled that out. Mental problem or not, he was stepping back in time or time was stepping back on him. Taking these little time strolls was actually kind of fun at times but who knew what the eventual outcome would be. They could very well prove harmful to his health. Perhaps the time involved would increase. Jason had no desire to live much of his life over again. Should he go back far enough though—he had little doubt that he would see to it that he was trained to be a plumber, electrician, or something of the sort. If this was all due to some mental problem then so be it. The whole affair was mind boggling. Was he the only person in the world with the time traveling "skill?" It would seem rather presumptuous to make that assertion but Jason had never heard of such a thing before except in time travel movies and books and there was always some kind of machine involved. Also he couldn't imagine a bunch of people running around and setting the world back by sixty seconds simultaneously.

That very night Jason did apprise Katy of his situation. She was understanding but insisted that his imagination was the culprit—that it had somehow been thrown out of whack by the trauma of losing his job. Her logic was reasonable—in fact she was entertaining

Chapter 4

Jason awakened early the next morning and waited anxiously for Katy to arise. He felt excited by the prospect of having someone who would believe him and share his burden. When Katy did get up, words begin pouring from his mouth at such a rate that she had to halt him and force him to restart—and to proceed at a slower pace. Jason forced himself to calm down. His plan was simple. Katy was to write something on a piece of paper and not reveal her message to him. Next Jason would ask her to tell him what she had written and she was to comply. Then Jason would concentrate on the word "NISS" and attempt to invoke a time slip. The fact that Katy had read him what she had written would be lost. Jason, however, would remember and thus prove that something strange had indeed happened when he told her the words. Katy thought the whole idea was ridiculous but, largely in order to please Jason, she complied and the experiment went just as planned. Katy argued that it had proved nothing and that Jason should continue to see the psychiatrist. She insisted that she didn't remember ever hearing Jason's instructions about writing on the paper. Only then did Jason realize the fact that only he could remember the incident. It was if it had never happened for everyone else. He tried the whole test again and this time was more careful with his timing. This time Katy remembered Jason's instructions to write on the paper but not the fact that he had then told her to read what she had written. Katy was now as puzzled as he was. Jason was greatly relieved to know that he was not entirely subject to involuntary time slips but that he could indeed also invoke the same of his own volition. At the same time he was glad to have an "accomplice" who understood what he was going through. Incidentally, Katy had written only two words on the note—"NISS sucks!" Jason couldn't help but remark that this was also his sentiment.

Jason went on to assure Katy that no one could be faulted for doubting him. Indeed it was doubtful whether anyone could believe him as he could scarcely believe the whole thing himself. Katy was scared but Jason himself was growing rather accustomed to the time slips. Jason then explained again what had happened and tried to form an analogy with which he got nowhere. Finally he compared the situation to an old phonograph record which one could play but which would sometimes skip backwards and play the same track or groove over again. Again there were countless questions to ask but no answers. What had caused him to develop that strange ability in the first place? Would the ability go away in time? Would 60 second always be the duration of the time slips? Why was he now able to apparently bring on the episode when desired? The questions went on and on with no answers.

Jason remembered a discussion in college about time. He didn't remember much of what had been said but he did recall that time is not the simple concept that people accepted. He would have to consult some books about the nature of time. Regardless of what he found he knew that he would have some valuable information to add.

Chapter 5

Jason's musing were interrupted as Jeff came back into the room after leaving the breakfast table to go the bathroom. Jason felt that there was now more to tell Jeff and began discussing the issue again. He told Jeff to sit. Jeff immediately assumed that he had done something wrong but Jason was quick to do away that notion. "No, Jeff," he said. "if anyone is wrong around here it's with me but I don't know what it is?"

He then went on to retell the story and left nothing out. Jeff's response to the whole affair was predicable. "Cool," he said.

The light response made Jason laugh. Perhaps he was taking the matter too seriously.

Next Jeff had his father repeat the note trick and was truly amazed when Jason recited his message which was much the same as Katy's had been except for the words. Jeff had written "Fuck NISS" which well expressed Jason's feelings also. Jason wanted to repeat the trick but Jeff was satisfied. Jason was encouraged by how quickly he was able to invoke the time slip this time. It was only a matter of concentrating on the magic word for a few seconds.

"Hey dad, I've got an idea," spoke up Jeff. If these things last for 60 seconds you could make some money in Las Vegas. Aren't we concerned with money right now?"

"We don't need money that bad," interjected Katy.

"Oh but we will in a month," replied Jason. "It doesn't look like I'm going to find a job anytime soon and we can't live on what you bring home. Maybe I could at least win enough to get us by for a while."

Katy was dead set against the plan—particularly since it involved Jason going by himself. "Well, take some time off and go with me," said Jason.

"I can't do that right now—we're too busy."

"Well, if we wait a month we'll be in a real financial bind," reminded Jason.

"I'll go with you, dad," chimed in Jeff.

"No you won't" interposed Katy. "You've got final exams next week and scholarships to think of."

Finally it was decided that Jason would have to indeed go alone. He would, however, call every night and check in. That decision having been made, Jason decided that a few preparations were in order. He went to a specialty store that he knew carried money belts. This was an item that you would never find in a JC Penny, Sears,or Woolworth outlet. He selected a belt that would accommodate a lot of bills—the advertisement stated that it would hold 10,000 dollars. Jason severely doubted this as even with hundred dollar denominations the belt would have to accommodate 1000 of the bills. It would be so thick by then that everyone would know that he was wearing a money belt anyway and the whole purpose would have been defeated. The problem was that the treasury had discontinued making bills larger than 100 dollars in 1969. If this were not the case the belt could have held a million dollars—one hundred $10,000 bills. Finally Jason decided to forego the belt altogether and simply purchased two small backpack—actually daypacks which would not look out of place for a vacationer. He had considered taking his attaché case but had seen too many movies with attaché cases that were filled with money. Two packs seemed to be overdoing it but Jason bought them anyway. A good sized fanny pack might have sufficed but Jason hated them—calling them "pseudo-colostomy bags."

Next Jason went to a gun shop, Big Al's Pistol and Rife Center. The store had a small shooting range for buyers who wanted to try out their weapons. He was aware of the fact that he would never be able to carry a sidearm while gambling in any casino, but this was not what he intended. He would leave the pistol in a back pack and put the backpack on the floor while he was playing or have it locked in a locker if they were available. The purpose of the weapon was to protect him while he wasn't gambling. He intended to wear a light sports jacket and would then be able to simply stick the gun in a coat pocket or in his belt for that matter as it would not be visible. He would also sleep with the gun. He was perhaps being overcautious because he did realize that he would probably he able to undo a robbery if such should occur merely by forcing a time slip. Nevertheless he wanted protection as he anticipated winning a lot of money. Jason already possessed 5 pistols but they were too large to serve his purpose. With Al's help he finally selected a Charter Arms .38 snub nosed 5 shot revolver. Five rounds should be plenty to discourage anyone with robbery on their mind and accuracy would certainly not be a problem. Jason took the gun to the range and was able to hit a 1 foot target at 30 feet 9 of 10 times. There was considerable kick but Jason was unfazed having shot a .45 automatic many time while in Vietnam. He had, in fact, killed two Viet Cong with the weapon. In addition he owned a .44 Magnum which kicked like a mule.

It was decided that Jason would leave the following morning. There was no use in procrastinating the matter. He gathered as much money as he could—depleting their checking account and taking whatever cash advances he could on their credit cards. In addition he withdrew the $10,000 they had in their savings account and which was intended for Jim's next tuition payment. This accomplished, he went to bed, intending to rise at 3:00 AM and depart. He hoped to be able to make the drive in one day even though the distance was about 900 miles. He calculated that some 15 hours would be required.

Before Jason knew it the alarm was buzzing and it was time to get up. Jason shaved and showered and was ready to go at 3 AM. Katy had also gotten up and fixed him some bacon and eggs. Jason found an old thermos bottle and filled it with fresh coffee. It was now time to leave and Jason kissed Katy good bye. She was in tears and Jason reassured her that everything would work out.

After an exhausting drive across Colorado, Wyoming and Utah he finally arrived in Los Vegas at 7 pm. He had made the drive in 14 ½ hours with stops for a couple of meals and gas. It was Sunday, May 29, 2005 and the day before Jason's birthday. His age would be 48—too young to retire unless he was either an army lifer or a police officer. Jason planned on spending several weeks in Vegas though he hadn't mentioned this to his family. For one thing, he didn't want to acquire his money so rapidly as to attract attention. He actually didn't consider himself a gambler although he did know the basics of most of the games. He had played Texas Hold'em on the Internet quite often and was always able to hold his own. With his 60 second replay ability it was difficult to imagine how he could possibly lose. However he certainly couldn't allow himself to win every hand.

Chapter 6

It was rather hot in Vegas but not really uncomfortable. One thing about Las Vegas—it was never humid or sticky—unlike the jungles of Vietnam 25 years earlier. It was just hot and dry. Jason was already missing Katy. They had made love the night before and Jason was still marveling at the intensity involved.

Jason began to formulate a plan. First of all he would try the slots. He would begin by inserting coins in a machine. Most of the machines now accepted bills also—unlike the old days. When he hit a jackpot he would slip back 60 seconds and redo the spin after betting the maximum amount. He planned to keep track of the last symbols displayed on the rightmost reels in order to know that a jackpot spin was coming. He might miss on occasion but he could always slip back again if necessary. He could handle Blackjack in much the same fashion. He didn't know much about playing craps but would learn. His favorite card game was Texas Hold'em and he planned to spend a lot of time at the tables. Roulette was one game that Jason was really counting on. He would watch one spin then slide back and redo his bet. He should be able to double his money simply by betting odd/even or red/black. He also planned to depend heavily on Keno. One problem with the latter game was that 60 seconds just wasn't enough for that game. He would possibly have to go back several minutes once he found out what numbers he needed to select. He conducted a little experiment that involved piggybacking time slips to see if this was possible. What this amounted to was invoking another time slip before the previous one had expired. With the help of his watch he determined that this was indeed possible. This meant that the amount of time he could go back was actually unlimited in a sense. He would age only 1 minute while performing multiple time slips.

Jason checked into a hotel on Fremont Avenue in the downtown area and got a decent room. He planned to live comfortably but not lavishly. He quickly took a shower and considered going out to gamble for while but decided that he was just too tired and to postpone his debut until the next morning. He finally decided to visit the store that he had noticed next to his hotel and purchase a bottle of vodka and some Collins mix. This done, he mixed himself a drink and thought about what lay ahead for him. He did have a swimming suit with him so he donned the suit and went down to the lobby area and the swimming pool. He didn't intend to do any swimming but did want to soak in the hotel's jetted hot pool. He made himself comfortable in the pool—too comfortable in fact as he dozed off and suddenly found his face underwater. He began sputtering and coughing as he looked around to see if anyone had been watching. Directly opposite him in the spa pool was a pretty girl who was laughing and obviously at him. He could nothing but laugh himself and try to explain. Soon he was engaged in a conversation with the young lady who proved to be a college student who was in Vegas with three friends for a week.

Jason slept until 5 AM which was about normal for him. The early morning hours were a good time to plan out the activities for the day as well as to contemplate whatever deserved to be contemplated. He considered the early morning hours as "his" time. At the present time Jason certainly had much to contemplate. He performed a series of push-ups and sit-ups and then went outside to jog for a mile. The fact that he was going to be living a somewhat decadent life for the next few weeks didn't mean that he should stop exercising. After his jog Jason showered and shaved. On this, Jason's 48th birthday, he decided to start out the day with a good breakfast—steak and eggs in fact. As he didn't intend to return to his room before beginning to gamble he put a roll of hundred bills in his pocket. He considered taking his backpack with the revolver along with him but finally decided against it. He wanted to investigate, first of all, to find out whether the casinos would allow him to retain a backpack while gambling. It seemed to him that this would be no different than allowing a woman to carry a purse. He suspected that the casinos would all have lockers where patrons could check their belongings but wanted to check on this. Perhaps he would also have to purchase a padlock.

Many of the casinos served very cheap or even free breakfasts but Jason was in the mood for something more substantial. As he passed the concierge's desk he asked the man where he could get a good steak and egg breakfast. The concierge replied that the restaurant right across the street was as good a place as any and Jason heeded his advice.

After a leisurely breakfast Jason walked the half block to the Golden Nugget casino where he planned to begin his day. He noted that some of the other gamblers carried backpacks so he walked back to his hotel and got one of his own along with the revolver which he thrust in the pack.

Seven AM found Jason back in the Golden Nugget where there were already many gamblers, many having stayed out all night to pursue elusive fortunes. Jason found a simple three reel slot machine where the top prize of $800 was paid to anyone who bet a dollar and then had the reels stop with red, white and blue 7s on a pay line. He inserted a 20 dollar bell and was thankful that the days of inserting nickels were gone. He went through the 20 without seeing a potential win on any line and he inserted a second bill. This time he noticed the needed 7s on the bottom line—a line that he hadn't selected. He then concentrated on his magic word—the name of his hated employer and stepped back in time where he waited for a cherry in each of the outside reel positions, a spin which had immediately preceded the spin with the three 7s. Once he saw the cherries he bet the maximum allowed which would cause the bottom line to be covered and hit the trip 7s. The machine made a hideous noise and Jason almost hit the floor—thinking he was back in Vietnam and the VC were trying out a new weapon. A casino employee shortly arrived and paid Jason his $800 in crisp new hundred dollar bills. Having had enough of the slots Jason then moved to an empty blackjack table.

The dealer seemed overly friendly which was often the case or so it seemed. The minimum bet was $5 and Jason played about even for a half hour and then told the dealer that he had to go. Before leaving he hit a 21 and noted that his previous hand had been 2,2. Now he simply forced his way back in time and waited for the 2,2. Once he had played that hand he bet 500 dollars on the next hand, collected his 750 dollars in winning chips and left the game. He proceeded to the cashier but cashed in only 500 dollars worth of chips. He had read that the IRS insisted on being informed about all cash-ins that amounted to 600 dollars or more. He considered the matter further and decided not to try and avoid the IRS. He wasn't being exactly patriotic but didn't want to bother to go to the cashier every time he neared the 600 dollars mark in winnings.

Next Jason decided to try some Texas Hold'em. He suddenly realized that the trip to Vegas had actually been unnecessary as he could have simply played hold'em on the Internet. He had done all right with this at home although he had never reached the point where he was able to request a withdrawal. However he reasoned that since he was in Vegas he might a well use the time beneficially.

The game was actually quite simple. The object was to create the best poker hand possible from 7 cards—2 hole cards and 5 community cards. Initially each player was dealt his two hole cards and a betting round ensued. Next three community cards were placed in the middle of the table and the players bet again. These three cards were called "the flop." The fourth community card, the "turn card," was then dealt and a third betting round took place. Following that round the "river card" came out and the final betting round began.

He found that the poker tables were in a separate large room at the Golden Nugget. Jason remembered reading about how Doyle Brunson, Amarillo Slim and some other guy had brought the game to Las Vegas in the 70s after inventing it in a small town in Texas. Within a short time it became very popular and was now called the "Cadillac of poker." Jason made a mental note to himself to find out when the next World Series of Poker event would take place.

On his way to the poker room Jason stopped at a roulette table. On a whim he bought some chips and put 100 dollars on the number 48, his newly achieved age. The wheel came up with a 26 so he forced a time slip and found the wheel had not yet been spun so he replaced his 100 dollars on the table but this time on number 26. In order to appear somewhat normal he placed a hundred dollars on each of four other numbers. When the wheel was spun and 26 was hit Jason tried his best to act excited but was not very successful. Oh well—he would have to practice.

It was now noon and Jason had been playing hold'em for four hours. He lost on occasion purposely but won perhaps too often as players kept leaving the table. He tried to avoid using time slips but resorted to them on occasion when he suspected a bluff. Even this didn't help when the bluffer failed to show his cards after a successful bluff. Jason found that he felt somewhat guilty about having used time slips during his hold'em session and decided to try and avoid this in the future. He didn't feel at all guilty about taking money from the casinos but didn't want to take unfair advantage of his fellow gamblers. He would try to avoid using time slips while playing hold'em and attempt to win with the skills that he had. However if he happened to end up in a one-on-one situation with a rude player he wouldn't hesitate to invoke a time slip and punish that player.

Jason found that he was now hungry and had a craving for some good Mexican food. He went back to his hotel and got in his car, intending to drive to the strip where he was told there were several good Mexican restaurants. He found one of the restaurants he had been told about. While waiting for his food Jason consumed a couple of large margaritas and was feeling no pain. He realized that he was going to have to watch himself or he would return home as a raging alcoholic.

For lunch Jason had 3 enchiladas, one cheese, one beef and one chicken. After more less inhaling his food he drove back to hotel and took a 2 hour nap. He felt good when he got up—the alcohol fortunately not affecting him. For the rest of the day Jason entertained himself by driving around the city and looking at the sights. It had been some ten years since he had been in Vegas and there had certainly been a lot of building going on. Among other destinations Jason drove out to the Hoover Dam on Lake Mead. The dam was just 30 miles southeast of the city so a short drive was required. At the time of its construction in the 30s it had been the largest dam in the world. Ninety-six men were killed during its construction. Jason paid the seven dollar fee and was able to actually go inside the dam which he found extremely interesting despite his preoccupation with gambling.

Jason spent the next two days on Fremont Street playing mostly hold'em at the Golden Nugget, the

Fremont, the Stratosphere, El Cortez and several other casinos. During his breaks from the hold'em tables he would play some blackjack or entertain himself at a roulette table. At the latter he bet mostly either red/black or odd/even. The fact that something was going on was just too evident when he placed a large sum on a single number. He began each day with an exercise session followed by a mile of jogging.

On Thursday Jason moved from his hotel to the Mirage on the strip. Before embarking to gamble he put $2,000 in his pocket to get him onto a hold'em table. Jason found that the Mirage itself seemed to be a good poker site. Over a period of 3 hours he won some $7,000 without using a time slap so he was quite satisfied and quit at 9 PM. He then cashed in his chips and visited the men's room where he deposited his cash in his backpack. After having the pack locked in a hotel he swam for a half—hour and soaked his aching muscles in a Jacuzzi. He couldn't understand why his muscles were sore and the best that he could come up with was that he had been unconsciously flexing various muscles—particularly those in his back and neck. He had been completely unaware of this and should probably try and avoid this "tell." Thus far he had run into no players who seemed to be experts. Now Doyle Brunson would undoubtedly note that Jason was unable to keep from tightening his muscles at certain times. He decided to avoid the downtown casinos for the remainder of his trip. The real money was in the behemoth casinos on the strip. These were so large and affluent that one customer's winnings couldn't phase them.

Friday was largely a repeat of the previous day. Jason played hold'em at Caesar's and several other large casinos and everything went according to plan. At about 4 PM he suddenly realized that he was famished—not having had anything to eat since breakfast at the Mirage. He found that he was in the mood for some good seafood. The concierge recommended a restaurant that was a little over two miles away—somewhat farther than Jason wanted to walk so he went to his room and got his car keys. He began driving through a rather seedy area of town. He was stopped at a light when a black male walked up to the passenger window with a revolver and demanded Jason's wallet. Jason concentrated on his magic word and the next thing he knew the man was just stepping off the curb. By the time he reached the open car window he was staring down the barrel of a .38 special. He groped for words and then stumbled away in confusion. Jason had simply drawn the gun from a jacket pocket. He had noted that a sports coat with levis was common attire in Vegas. Jason wasn't carrying that much money but he still didn't intend to robbed.

Finally he entered the restaurant and took a seat near the exit and facing the entrance. Perhaps he had watched too many westerns where the heroic gunfighter did the same thing but he did feel safer that way. A waitress brought him a menu and he was surprised at the large selection. Then the cook himself came out and asked if he could be of assistance. Jason was a little overwhelmed and asked the cook what he would recommend. The cook told Jason, that if he liked swordfish, he couldn't go wrong with that selection. Jason had indeed had swordfish steak on one occasion and liked it very much so he opted for that selection.

Although the restaurant was quite busy, Jason's food arrived in minutes and was so hot that he had to wait for a few minutes to begin eating. Once he did begin all else was forgotten. The steak was far superior to the one he had had previously. Whereas that one had been good it had also been a little chewy. This one melted in Jason's mouth. After finishing the last bite he left a generous tip and waved to the chef whom he could see in the half open cooking area.

On the drive back to the Mirage Jason placed the revolver on the passenger seat so that it would be handy. He rolled up all the windows, relying on the car's air conditioner which didn't seem to be quite up to the task. He arrived at the hotel without incident, got some ice, and mixed up a vodka collins. Jason realized that it was now 8 PM at home as he was now on Pacific time. He had promised to call home every night and he now fulfilled that duty. Katy sounded worried and was happy to know that things were going well. Of course Jason did not tell her about the robbery attempt. She had no idea that he had a gun with him and would certainly have done all she could to prevent him from bringing it with him in the first place. Jeff was a different matter but Jason still didn't mention the incident. Jeff wanted to know every detail regarding Jason's experiences. His concluding words were "Cool dad—see if you can bankrupt the strip. Those places have too much money anyway." Jason couldn't help but agree.

He was tired but his mind was racing and sleep eluded him. He finally put a finger on what was bothering him. What lay in the future for him? Could anyone live as he was living? If he were to die what would become of his family? In the middle of these questions Jason reached a conclusion. Originally he had come to Las Vegas to get money to get by on until he could find a job. His thought had been that he could always return to the city if necessary. Perhaps they could even move to Las Vegas. Now Jason was looking at things somewhat differently. First of all he might never find a job. There was also no telling when the time slips were leading him. He didn't know how long they would last nor what they were doing to him. Everything pointed to one conclusion—he had to take advantage of the here and now to take care of his family for life. This meant retiring all debt as well as accumulating a considerable sum for the future. Frankly, Jason never wanted to have to worry about money again. He would add up the money he made thus far and pay taxes on it. It wasn't worth it to attempt to outwit the IRS.

Giving up on sleep, he went to the hotel's guest computer and began reading about the strip. Based on information from one site he compiled a list of all the casinos on the strip and decided to hit 3 of them a day. His list read:

1. Aladdin
2. Barbary Coast
3. Boardwalk
4. Bourbon Street
5. Caesar's Palace
6. Circus Circus
7. Ellis Island
8. Excalibur
9. Flamingo
10. Frontier
11. Hard Rock Café

12. Harrrah's
13. Hotel San Reno
14. Imperial Palace
15. Klondike Inn
16. Luxor
17. Mandalay Bay
18. MGM Grand
19. Mirage
20. Greek Ilses
21. Monte Carlo
22. New York New York
23. Psalms
24. Paris
25. Rio
26. Rivera
27. Royal
28. Sahara
29. Stardust
30. Stratasphere Tour
31. Terribles
32. Treasure Island
33. Tropicana
34. Tuscany
35. Venetian
36. Westin Casino
37. Westward Ho
38. Wynn

The list was somewhat outdated and some of the casinos were out of business. Also some of the newer ones weren't listed. It was now 11 PM but Jason still felt incapable of sleeping. He finally decided to undertake one more session of gambling but first decided to mix himself a vodka collins. As his ice was melted he first grabbed the small bucket and exited his room. He rounded a corner and was heading for the ice machine when he heard a scream from down the hallway. "He's got my purse!" an attractive lady in an evening gown cried.

Jason ran to her side and asked where the assailant had gone as no one else was visible. "The elevator!" she cried and Jason looked to her side where the elevator was located and had just departed. Noting that it was going down he opened the door to the stairway and started down—taking two steps at a time. He wasn't sure where the man would exit but assumed that he would go to the ground floor. He burst out of the stairwell just as the elevator opened but it was empty. Jason now realized that only a time slip would enable him to catch the thief. Quickly he concentrated on the initials of his hated former employer and found that he was now back in his room. The previous time he had taken a minute to put on a shirt but realized now that he didn't have time. He thought about repeating the slip but then said to himself, "oh what the hell! This isn't a dinner engagement." Quickly he grabbed the metal bucket and emerged shirtless into the hallway. He turned the corner just in time to see a man grab a purse from the lady and spring into a waiting elevator. Jason reached the elevator just as the doors were closing and burst through, slamming the ice bucket into the man's face. The man fell back against the wall and Jason quickly planted a foot into his genitals. As the man bent over in pain Jason repeated the blow with the bucket and connected with his forehead. The man collapsed on the elevator floor just as the doors were closing. Quickly

39

Jason pushed the "open" button and the doors reopened to reveal the anxious victim of the robbery. Jason handed her the purse with a smile and said "I think this belongs to you." As she was thanking him a hotel security guard arrived and told them that he would take care of things and notify the police.

After this singular interlude Jason found himself a bit shaken as he retrieved his now misshapen ice bucket. For the second time he headed for the ice machine and then returned to his room where he mixed the drink for which he was now more than ready.

He then decided to try another of the casinos on his list. They would undoubtedly have some high stakes hold'em games and he needed some experience at the latter. Before coming to Vegas he had never before played for stakes other than nickels, dimes or quarters online. Finally Jason decided to visit Caesar's Palace one more time. He was happy to see that a large number of high stakes games were going on. He decided to play five card stud instead of hold'em in order to determine at what game he could make the most money in the shortest amount of time. He played for several hours without even invoking a time slip and was doing quite well. Jason had always been a decent poker player but the big difference now was that he could bluff without worrying about losing. He was also in a position to call any suspected bluffs. Basically he was the best player there so he chose to play without the time slips as he had planned to do anyway. When he finally left the game he was up by $3,000. At 1:30 AM Jason walked back to the Mirage and went to bed. This time he went quickly to sleep.

Chapter 7

The next morning Jason packed up his suitcase and threw it into the trunk of his BMW. He retrieved his backpacks from the hotel safe and then checked out. He had discovered that the Aladdin had rooms for half the price he was paying at the Mirage. Although he could well afford to stay wherever he wanted he didn't want to become totally frivolous. He might as well save money whenever possible. The Aladdin was also the first casino on his list so he might as well start out his playing there and tackle the casinos in order. He would skip Caesars as he had already taken close to $20,000 from them. Before he went to his room he checked out the casino at the Aladdin. It was enormous. It seemed like the Internet had mentioned something to the effect that Aladdin had 100,000 square feet of casino space.

Jason was impressed by his room and even more impressed by the fact that there were 2500 such rooms. The place was like a small city. It contained seven restaurants so there would really be no need to go elsewhere for food. Jason felt the need for immediate action so he unpacked his suitcase. First off he headed for the roulette tables. After losing several hundred dollars he placed 100 dollars on his number, 48. The wheel was spun and the little ball ended up on the 11. Jason then did his time slip and now placed his 100 dollar chip on the 11. He then placed hundred dollar chips at random on 5 other numbers. As the dealer shoved him the chips he took off his baseball hat, a Yankee hat, as he had always idolized Babe Ruth, Lou Gehrig, Mickey Mantle and especially Yogi Berra who had a nonpareil way with words. He pushed his chips into the hat and headed for the cashier. He cashed in for 36 hundred dollars and filled out his form for the IRS.

Now Jason went to a blackjack table where he was the only player. He played conservatively for a while not even bothering with time slips. Finally he decided it was time to get busy so he upped his bets to $100. He lost one hand, won one and then the next two as he invoked time slices. He then avoided any more time manipulation for a half hour. Finally he then became bored and told the dealer that he was "all-in." The dealer laughed and said, "We're not playing Texas Hold'em here as he dealt Jason a pair of aces. These would have been a great hand in hold'em but were also good in blackjack. Of course in blackjack the cards needed to be split and the bet doubled. This was exactly what Jason did and was rewarded by two face cards that gave him two 21s. The dealer turned over his card and had to stop dealing as he had a king and an 8. "There's a $500 dollar table in the high roller room if you really want to make some big bets," he advised. Jason thanked him and left a nice tip while asking for directions to the room. Jason now proceeded to the high roller room. Soon he reached a roped-off area where an employee asked him if he was really going to play—that observers weren't welcome. "I'm a player" replied Jason and meant it in more ways than one as he intended to play with time. "Well then welcome to my abode," said the guard.

Jason immediately felt underdressed as many of the players were dressed in suits and the casino personnel wore tuxedos. He then noticed that were also players in shorts which made him feel overdressed in his levis, golf shirt and sports jacket. Most of the games that were going on were Baccarat—a game that Jason had never played. He knew just the fundamentals. The idea was to get nine in two card. This was a natural win. Eight was also a natural win and could only be beaten by nine. It you went over nine you could take another card. If you ended up with a 17 or whatever the one would be dropped. Face cards counted as 10 and aces as 1. Jason didn't understand the betting so he watched a hand. Apparently only two participants received cards—these were known as the banker and the player and the remaining participants bet on the cards of these two. Jason took a seat and tossed $500 on the table. He had seen this done and the cashier quickly swooped in and converted the money to chips.

After a half hour Jason was up by $10,000 even though he still didn't understand many things about the game. Some of the others were laughing at him but this didn't bother him in the slightest and he laughed right along with them. He saw that exact amount being wagered by a gentleman in a suit. However the guy lost the bet and Jason decided not to push his neither his luck nor his incipient time traveling abilities. He quit the table and tipped the dealer a hundred dollars. From there he went to the cashier to cash in his chips and fill out his accustomed IRS form.

As he headed for the casino exit to the hotel he passed the Keno area. He hadn't yet tried the game and decided it was about time he did so. Just going back 60 seconds wouldn't buy him anything. He would have to perform multiple time slips in order to have time to fill out a new card before the numbers started coming out. He had found out that he could actually slide back in time more than 60 seconds by simply invoking time slips one after another. After several tries he finally won a $15,000 jackpot. It was somewhat difficult to remember 15 numbers but Jason had always had a good memory. He then continued for the exit but stopped at a roulette table. He repeated his efforts of the previous day and walked away with 3600 dollars. The casino employee in charge of the game looked at Jason as if had been cheating but Jason merely said, "Can you believe that luck."

Chapter 8

By now Jason was ready for lunch and decided to try one of the Aladdin's seven restaurants. First however, he wanted to get one of his backpacks from the hotel safe and empty his pockets. He did so and while he was it, asked the concierge for his recommendation as to where he should have lunch. He heeded the forthcoming advice and had a light but delicious lunch which featured smoked chicken strips which were very tender and tasty. Following lunch Jason played the slot machines. He found the most expensive machine he could and then played the least amount he could until hitting a big jackpot. Then he would invoke a time slip and make his bet as large as allowable. After winning a large jackpot he suddenly heard a voice behind him. "How do you know when you're going to hit a big jackpot? It seems like that's the only time you bet big money."

Jason turned and saw a pleasant looking man with sandy colored hair. "I guess I just have a feel for it," he said.

"You ought to try the big money machines," said the sandy haired one." They're roped off in the corner back there so you'll feel special. You notice how they offer us drinks out here. In the corner you'll get a new drink before you finish your old one."

Jason shook hand with the man as they introduced themselves. The guy's name was, appropriately enough, Sandy. "Let's see if my magic works for you," said Jason.

He then had the man spin the reels on the slot machine until he hit a decent jackpot on a line that wasn't selected. "It's going to hit next spin," said Jason." Put 10 dollars in this time."

Sure enough the machine hit a 500 dollar jackpot. Sandy insisted on sharing the jackpot with Jason but Jason would have none of that. "Let's hook up later for a drink" said Jason as he headed for the roped off area in the corner. The slot machines there were just what Jason was looking for. The minimum on one machine was $100 and the maximum was $500. The jackpots were astronomical. An hour later Jason was $50,000 richer and no one had bothered him except waitresses who wanted to bring him drinks. As he was leaving Sandy came up. Jason hailed him and they walked to the nearest bar together. Sandy was a lawyer from Arizona. He was divorced and going to be town for a week. Jason told Sandy about his plan to make the rounds of the various casinos in Vegas and invited him to come along whenever he could. "Today is Tuesday," Jason said. I'm going to spend the rest of the day here at the Aladdin. Tomorrow I'm going to hit the MGM Grande, the Tropicana and New York New York. Thursday it'll be the Excalabur, the Luxor and Mandalay Bay. Friday will be the Monte Carlo, Boardwalk and the

Bellagio. After that I've got at least 25 places in mind but I'll play them before I leave. I've got at least 2 weeks if I need them.

"From what I've seen you'll be a millionaire before the week is out," commented Sandy.

"That's just what I had in mind," responded Jason with a smile.

Jason was tired—tired from the exertion of forcing time slips so he returned to his room for a nap. Although he was on the 10th floor it was easy to get to the lobby or the casino. The hotel was arranged so that no room was farther than 7 rooms from an elevator. Jason slept for about 2 hours and awoke bright-eyed and refreshed. He planned on getting in a high stakes poker game that evening but first he wanted a good steak. He phoned Sandy's room to see if he was hungry. Sandy replied that he was indeed hungry and that he was ready to go so the two of them planed to meet in the lobby in 5 minutes Once there, they asked the concierge for advice and he recommended a place that was within walking distance. They took the short walk and were rewarded with a couple of excellent steaks. As they ate they talked and Jason learned that Sandy also had children in college—both at the University of Arizona, a girl who was majoring in nursing and a son in law school. Sandy himself had been divorced for just over 6 months and had custody of the kids. He was taking a week off before beginning a case that would probably last for several months. He liked to gamble but said he was too cheap to lose very much.

Upon returning to the Mirage Jason was ready for some high stakes poker. He was almost immediately involved in one of these. The minimum bet was 100 dollars and some of the bets were enormous. Jason amused himself by trying to play without time slips. Now that he could afford to do this he found it very entertaining. He didn't mind cheating the casinos but he didn't like doing this to his fellow poker players. This might well be spurious reasoning but it was the way Jason felt. He did enjoy the camaraderie of most of the other players.

When the night was done Jason was up by just over $30k and had enjoyed a great time. There were also other winners but they did not begrudge Jason his victories and no one had outdone him—he was proud of that fact. He vowed to do the rest of his poker playing in this fashion. He would use his time slips when he was pitted only against the house.

Chapter 9

The rest of the week consisted of some grueling days for Jason. He was often accompanied by Sandy but the latter shied away from the high stakes games that Jason actively sought out. Jason did take time to gamble with Sandy but didn't force him to use take advantage of a times time slip. Sandy was already suspicious and might have intuited what was going on. One new game Jason attempted was craps. He hadn't even taken the time to learn the rules of the game. One problem was that it seemed that the bets were too small to interest him. He didn't like to bet too much more than the other gamblers. For this reason he was doing most of gambling in the high roller rooms. Most of the casinos had high stakes no limit table Texas hold'em tables in the high stakes area. Limit hold'em or pot limit hold'em didn't interest him at all. A big bet on a no-limit table was not at all out of place—in fact it was the norm.

Jason finally made a decision but was afraid it would leave Sandy out of the picture to a large extent. He wanted to get his money amassed and be done with it. Then he would be able to relax and have fun without having to worry about time slips. To this end he began hurrying from casino to casino—seeking the high roller rooms or the elite slot machines. On Wednesday Jason and Sandy visited the MGM Grande, the Tropicana, and New York New York. On Thursday they had breakfast together and Jason told Sandy of what he had in mind. To Jason's surprise Sandy still wanted to accompany him.

"I wanted to see Vegas and that's what I'll be doing," he said. "I can always find something to entertain myself while you do your high rolling."

"Well let's get moving," said Jason. "I've got a car and I think we'll take it today."

The entire day was spent on the move and the duo hit the Excaliber, the Luxor, the Mandalay, the Orleans, the Monte Carlo the Boardwalk and the Bellagio. Jason left a backpack in the car and they twice had to make trips to Jason's BMW to empty Jason's pockets into the backpack which he kept locked in the trunk. They were very surreptitious about this with Sandy standing guard to ensure that no one saw what they were doing. Car trunks were just not all that safe from a determined burglar. By the time they finished for the day all of Jason's pockets had hundred dollar bills crammed into them. Back at the Alladin Jason took care of the money and he and Sandy then went out to eat. Jason insisted up on buying though Sandy protested. "You don't know how much money I made today and I'm not going to tell you," said Jason.

"I know how many trips we made to your car so you could empty your pockets," responded Sandy. After a late supper Jason headed for the Luxor again with

Sandy tagging along. This time he tried playing without the benefit of any time slips. It didn't seem to matter because he soon found himself up by $12,000. Perhaps he could play poker for a living if nothing else worked out. Jason already had plans to sign up for a World Series of Poker in a few months.

The next day, which was Friday, Jason and Sandy hit the Palms, the Gold Coast, the Rio, Casesar's Palace, and Treasure Island. Jason was immensely successful and began to think of going home. He was tired of the concentration needed to force one time slip after another.

After they had completed the circuit Jason invited Sandy to his room. Before doing so he had retrieved his other backpack from the hotel safe. Now he dumped all of the money on the bed and then dove in and began wallowing in hundred dollar bills. Sandy had a camcorder and filmed the episode while promising to copy the footage to a DVD and send it to Jason. Jason had no DVD player but would certainly buy one now. He was like a kid in a sandbox as he grabbed handfuls of bills and let them fall on his head. It was something that he had always wanted to do. Once, as a child, he had actually done this with 1 dollar bills. He could scarcely believe that he was now doing it with hundred dollar bills. Feeling somewhat foolish he now got up and set about organizing the money. He started making stacks on the table but was soon forced to the floor. Most of the bills were hundred dollars but there were also bills of smaller denominations. Jason opened a box of oversized rubber bands that they had picked up during the day and began making packages of the money. As he packaged he counted and found his grand total to be 565,225 dollars—not bad at all.

Once he was finished with the money and it was back in a backpack, Jason called Katy. He told her that he "half way there." She wanted to know what "half way" meant but he was elusive saying only that the job was half done.

Jason suspected that Sandy might be tiring of the frenetic pace he was setting and stated so at breakfast on Saturday morning. "Just hurry up and eat," said Sandy. "We've got a lot of places to go today. By the way, I am up by $5,000 for the trip so I'm not complaining nor asking for any help which I know you would give me if I were to ask."

"You've got that right," stated Jason. "The first place I've to got to go today is Western Union and wire some of money out of here and to my bank."

Sandy just shook is had, "I'm just amazed that you haven't been blacklisted yet." I still don't know how you do it. You say it's just a feeling that tells you what to do?"

"That's about it," said Jason though he longed to share his secret. At that time only Katy, Jeff and Jim knew of the time slips. Jason had cautioned them all to tell no one of his "affliction"—not that anyone would believe them anyway. Suddenly Jason felt the need to share with Sandy. Already they had formed a fast friendship and Jason felt instinctively that Sandy was to be trusted.

"All right, Sandy," he announced. "I want to show you something. Take this sheet of paper and write a few words on it. Then wait for a minute and then show me the paper."

"But then you'll know what I wrote," protested Sandy. "What's that going to show?"

"Just trust me and do it," insisted Jason and Sandy scribbled something on the paper. He paused for a minute or so and then showed the paper to Jason. Jason read the words that Sandy had written and then forced a time slip. He then sat back and resumed eating.

A few minutes later Sandy asked, "When are you going to ask me to show you the paper?"

I already did and it says, "Jason is wacko," laughed Jason. "So now you know how I'm winning—I'm basically a cheat," he continued.

"You're just using your God—given abilities. It's not your fault if you use what's given you, "responded Sandy.

Jason went on to tell Sandy about the high roller poker games and how he had gradually learned that he didn't need to travel backwards time in order to win.

"You don't have to do that but it's admirable that you do" commented Sandy. "As for the casinos fuck them—they fuck everone else."

"As for God, I haven't a clue as to how he's in the picture?" questioned Jason.

"I think you'll find out when the time comes," commented Sandy.

The two of them went on to discuss religion for a while among other things. Soon the two of them left the Aladdin. This time they drove as the Western Union station which was some distance away. Jason retained just $25,000 to play with and sent half a million home. Once he had taken care of this chore Jason threw the empty backpacks in the trunk and put the remaining $25,000 in his pockets. While they had the car Jason decided to visit the casinos at the far end of the strip. They parked at Circus Circus and spent about two hours there. Then they moved on to the Stratospher Tower, the Sahara the Riveria and the Hilton. At the Hilton they ate a well deserved and late lunch. After eating they had a drink and relaxed for a while. Sandy admitted that he was running low on cash, having sent $5000 to his bank account while they were at the Western Union station. Jason suggested that they get in a low stakes hold'em game and Sandy would signal Jason whenever a time slip was in order. After an hour of play Sandy told Jason that he was "good" and the dealer wanted to know what they were talking about. Sandy laughed and replied that he simply felt good—and he wasn't lying.

"Just tell me when you need some more," said Jason.

"Maybe tomorrow," answered Sandy.

Jason and Sandy spent the rest of Saturday at Westward Ho and Stardust. Jason found himself getting somewhat greedy in the higher roller rooms. Again he had to empty his pockets. He noticed that he felt a lot more secure now that a half million dollars was waiting for him at home and lost several big hands intentionally.

They had just arrived at Jason's car when two men got out of a car about 30 feet away from them. They approached Jason and Sandy rapidly and there was something threatening about them. Jason began to fumble for his .38 but it was buried beneath the money in his backpack which was hanging by a strap from his shoulder. "Okay, gentleman," one of the men said—a large Afro American with huge biceps which he displayed via a muscle shirt. "Time to pay the piper."

Before Jason had time to act Sandy was in motion. A spinning back kick from Sandy laid the man on the asphalt. The second man lunged at Sandy but the latter simply moved and chopped at the man's neck sending him sprawling. "Let me have him," interjected Jason. "Can't let you have all the fun."

The second man got up shakily and threw a punch at Jason which he easily avoided. He threw two sharp left jabs and followed these with a straight right that rendered the man unconscious. "Very nice," praised Sandy. "Where did you learn that?"

I was light heavy-weight champion of Scofield barracks in Hawaii after I got out of Vietnam" replied Jason. "And where did you learn that kick by the way."

Well, I'm the reigning karate champion of Phoenix for my age," returned Sandy.

Once they arrived at the Aladdin that night, Jason got his backpack from the trunk of the BMW. He then went to the room and found that his take for the day was a respectable $240,000. Almost everything was hundred dollar bills. After visiting the office and having his backpack locked up he called Katy. He told her that he had wired some money and that she could check the account balance the next morning. He refused to tell how much was the account but did say that she would be pleasantly surprised. She wanted to know when he would be back. He said simply that it would not be that much longer. He reassured her that he was fine—just tired and ready to come home.

"Just come home," she said. "We'll be okay."

The idea was very tempting. Jason now had over $800,000—even after taxes he would be able to eliminate their indebtedness including the house mortgage. With the remainder of the money and Katy's income they could live comfortably. The one factor that augured against going home was the boys' education. Jim had still had at least one year remaining and Jeff would be entering college in a year. The latter had good grades but they couldn't count on a scholarship. Then there was also the possibility that

Jim might want to go on to graduate school. Still thinking of his family and missing them Jason went to sleep.

Chapter 10

Jason awakened early and was ready to go by the time Sandy showed up for breakfast. "You may want to back off today, Sandy," said Jason in lieu of "good morning." I'm going to be going like hell. My goal is leave for home tomorrow—in fact right after I get you on a plane."

Sandy had already informed Jason that he was flying out the next day "Well, first of all you don't have to worry about getting me on a plane," said Sandy. "That's what taxis are for. Secondly I don't have anything else to do today anyway so I might as well chase after you as anything else."

"I'm going to push today so I may get us kicked out of some places," warned Jason.

"No, you'll get kicked out but I'll just leave on my on," corrected Sandy. "I'm not going into any of those high roller rooms with you.

Their plan for the day was simply to hit as many casinos as possible. They would start with 7 casinos that were almost in a row: Wyans's resort, the Venetian, the Imperial Palace, the Flamingo, Barbary Coast and

Bourbon Street. If they spent time at all of these casinos they would have put in a good day's work. They drove that day as some of the casinos were sometimes almost a block apart.

From the very start Jason was true to his word. He went for the jugular and made it clear that he was out to gamble. He still forced himself to lose some pots but not as many as normal. He was actually asked to leave two establishments but by that time the damage had been done and he was far ahead of the game. By noon he had emptied his pockets four times and the backpack was bulging. They drove back to the Aladdin for lunch and a quick nap. Jason, however, found that he was too pumped up to sleep and went down to Aladdin's casino. After emptying his pockets for the fifth time and performing a quick count as he transferred the money to his backpack. Jason found that he had made over $300,000 that day. This was a record and he still had lots of time to play.

Jason had planned to let Sandy sleep but a knock on his hotel door came while Jason was transferring the money to his backpack. Since Jason didn't really know if this was Sandy he opened the door with his .38 in hand. Sandy stepped back and laughingly asked Jason not to shoot him. "Take it easy, dirty Harry!" he exclaimed.

Since this would be their last chance Jason urged Sandy to let him help out with some timely time slipping. Sandy objected saying, "I don't really need more money.—after all I am a lucrative layer. You take care of yourself."

That afternoon they began with the Imperial palace where Jason was a killer. He was afraid that he would be asked to leave but it didn't happen. Once again his strategic losses came to his rescue or so he came to believe. Sandy was all excited because he had experienced a run of luck at a blackjack table. "You should have seen me, Jason," he exclaimed. "I was just like you."

Next they moved on to the Flamingo—the Barbary Coast and finally Bourbon Street. When they had finished their work at these casinos Jason was ready to call it quits. It was 4:00 in the afternoon and Jason figured that if they hurried they get the backpack from the hotel and make it to the Western Union station before they closed. He wanted the money out of sight and on its way to his checking account. The traffic was a problem but they finally made it back to the Aladdin. Jason did a quick count and found that he had some $750,000 to follow the half million he had already sent. Even after taxes he should have close to a million dollars. He could also deduct a large sum for gambling losses if desired. Hurriedly they got back in the car and reached the Western Union station just as it was about to close. Jason sent all of his money except for $5,000 which he needed to play one last session of high roller Texas Hold'em. In addition he still needed to pay for the room and required some money for the trip home.

As they drove back to the Aladdin Jason felt a great sense of relief. The pressure was off—not only the pressure to win but the pressure to make financial ends meet. He still needed, or at least wanted a job but this was no longer a pressing need. If what Sandy said was true and there were indeed jobs in Arizona he might well move there. Katy could actually retire as could Jason for that matter. He and Katy had always liked Arizona anyway—particularly after visiting the Grand

Canyon shortly before Jim was born. It was only NISS that had kept them in Colorado. Many people hated the heat of Arizona but Jason thrived on it. A swimming pool would be almost a necessity but both Jason and Katy loved to swim. A great deal depended upon where Jeff would go to college. Jason wasn't sure if his mind was really set on the University of Denver or if he were just intentionally trying to keep down college expenses. Jim had two semesters left but was not sure whether or not he wanted to enroll in graduate school.

That night Jason and Sandy ate at the Hard Rock Café and the food was surprisingly good. After they finished Sandy wanted to visit the Hard Rock casino and Jason didn't mind. He decided to make this his last session—win or lose. He sat at a blackjack table for several hours but ended up losing a hundred dollars as he didn't make use of his time traveling abilities.

As he left the table Sandy walked up laughing. "The dealer doesn't have a clue as to how lucky he is," he said.

Exhausted by their marathon day Jason and Sandy drove back to the Aladdin and were soon in bed. Sandy had to be at the airport by 9:00 AM and Jason insisted, of course, upon driving him.

Chapter 11

Jason arose at 6:00 AM and then shaved and showered. He wanted to make sure to get Sandy to the airport in plenty of time. Sandy was ready and they found themselves in a position to have a somewhat leisurely breakfast. Little was said as they ate. Both felt that a blossoming friendship was coming to an end. Once they reached the airport they were talking and Jason walked with his friend into the terminal building. After Sandy had checked his sole suitcase Jason continued the conversation. "You know, Katy and I have always loved Arizona."

"People always seem to like it if they can deal with the heat," said Sandy.

"I guess what I'm saying," continued Jason, "is that it's not beyond the realm of possibility that we might move down there—especially if I can find a job. Katy had pretty much find a job anywhere there's a hospital."

"Well, I sure would be happy to have you as a neighbor," said Sandy," and I'll look around and see what's available as far as jobs. I know quite a few people

61

in the industry including some former clients. Mail me a copy of your resume when you get a chance." The two had already exchanged phone numbers and Email addresses and promised each other to keep in touch.

When the time came to board the plane, Jason found himself nearly in tears as he embraced Sandy. "You have a safe flight," was all he could say.

"And you have a safe drive," countered Sandy.

As Jason pulled away he felt truly alone. He stuck a CD in the player and began the long drive home—in fact a 16 hour drive at 50 mph. Jason calculated that he could make it in 13 hours even stopping for gas and something to eat. Back in the old days he would have attempted to make the drive in a single day so as to avoid the expense of a motel room. Now he no such worry. The oil, radiator and tires all seemed to be in good condition. The BMW might be 10 years old but it had always provided good dependable transportation.

All went well until Jason reached the barren stretch in Utah between Beaver and Nephi. He caught himself dozing off several times and finally stopped at a rest area where he did several wind sprints. This was a tactic he had used with success in the past.

This time, however, the measure didn't seem to work and Jason decided he would have to take a short nap. Just as he neared an overpass he suddenly found himself veering off the freeway and into an open field. His first thought was that he was going to roll. Then he was back on the freeway and wide awake. He was sufficiently frightened at what might have been that he no longer needed to stop for a nap. The time slip had done its thing again and Jason was saved. This was now twice that the time slips had saved his life. Jason vowed that this would be the last time. He could not count on the slips to save his life again. He suddenly had a new thought. Perhaps everyone was going through time slips but couldn't remember them. For instance another driver might have dozed off and left the road. However he would be totally unaware of this and would therefore be doomed to repeat the mistake.

As Jason continued to drive he contemplated the time slips further. It was obvious that he was seeing just a tiny percentage of them. What was the overall cumulative effect of them? Must not earth's time be slowing down to accommodate the time slices. In other words must not a man be older than his established age due to the myriad of sixty second redos. He had not noticed a clock during a slip nor had he looked at his watch and wondered if the hands had jumped backward. Did this make any difference anyway?

The countless questions were driving Jason crazy and he did his bet to think about something else. He pictured Katy's face when she called the bank today to check out their balance. Of course she might get the same information from the Internet and would most likely do this. He pictured letters from his credit companies with payment due of $0.00 and could hardly restrain a laugh. He went on to picture himself going through their liabilities folder and paying off everything in full. He then pictured Jeff's animated face as Jason told him about playing with high rollers. With such thoughts he finally rolled into Salt Lake City and concluded his first day on the road. He got a room at a Comfort Inn—a motel chain that he liked. He then went next door and had a dinner of liver and onions which really "hit the spot."

At 6 AM the next morning Jason was once again on the road. He first stopped at a gas station and filled the BMW and also purchased a new thermos which he filled with coffee. He wasn't hungry so he didn't bother with breakfast even though the motel offered a free meal. He did however grab an apple and a banana. This time he was on the home stretch and the miles flew by quickly. At 12:30 PM he took the exit for Thornton and, in a matter of minutes was pulling into his driveway. Katy came running out to greet him and they embraced passionately.

"I was so worried about you," said Katy. "You could have been robbed or who knows what."

"I was fine the whole time," explained Jason. I made a friend and we spent almost the whole time together."

Katy wanted to know all about Sandy and Jason was more than willing to tell her all about him. "You two will have to stay in touch," she said. "Good friends are hard to come by."

"I hope to do more than just talk on the phone with him," said Jason somewhat mysteriously." but we'll talk about that later. Have you got any coffee on—that's what I need," he continued. "Then I've got some bills to pay."

Chapter 12

"Hey Katy—did you ever call the bank said Jason" the next morning as she fixed breakfast. She was taking a day of vacation as she wanted to spend the day with Jason.

"No," she replied. "All I've been doing is worrying about you."

"Well call them. You might be surprised at what I've made."

"Well, I hope it's enough to pay that stack of bills on the table," said Katy. "That'll take quite a wad of cash right there. Anyway the bank's not open yet but I can go online and check on our account. I got us set up for online banking last week. I've been going to do that for a long time but I haven't tried it yet".

Katy went upstairs to the study to get on the computer and Jason sat back to wait. A moment later Katy came downstairs with a look of disgust on her face." Our account is all screwed up, "she said. They're trying to tell me that we have something over a million dollars in it. I just wish we did—we'd pay off everybody and have all kinds of money left over."

"Well, let's start paying those vultures off," said Jason, "because that figure is right."

Katy let out a shriek and threw her arms around Jason's neck. "How did you do it?" she said over and over.

"I think I pushed my luck a little, replied Jason. "We'll take Jeff and go out and celebrate tonight."

Jason ate some pancakes and bacon and then cleared the table and sorted through the stack of bills. Then he went up to the study and retrieved the contents of a folder he called "current liabilities." What he ended up with was quite an imposing stack of bills. He began by paying the current household bills—telephone, water electricity, natural gas, newspaper, cell phone and cable TV. The next thing he did was to fetch all 5 of their credit cards. As they were all at their limit neither of them carried the cards. Jason found a matching bill for each card among the stack on the table. He took them one by one and made a payment—not the minimum amount due but the entire amount that was owed on the card. Katy enjoyed this very much and sat by with scissors to cut up each card as Jason finished with it. After Jason finished with the credit cards he located the home equity loan statement. It had a total amount of $75,000 outstanding and Jason quickly wrote out a check to cover that amount. He considered paying off the house but decided to wait until they had a chance to talk about possibly moving to Arizona.

For his next order of business Jason needed the telephone. He called to get the payoff amount for the boy's automobiles. The BMW was paid off. He then paid off the boys' cars. Katy's Suburu Outback came next and Jason wrote a check for just over $9,000 for that vehicle.

By now the stack of bills on the table had shrunk to nothing and instead that were a pile of receipts with each item marked "Paid."

"Well, now that you've paid everything in sight, do you think that we can afford a few groceries," said Katy.

"I think we can manage that, "replied Jason, "and I think I could use a home-cooked meal. We'll go out tomorrow night."

"Another thing we've got to do tonight is to call Jim, "said Katy. "We've got so much to tell him. I didn't tell you but I guess there's a chance that he might be getting his scholarship back. The professor who disqualified him is all kinds of trouble."

Jason and Katy spent a quiet but enjoyable afternoon together. They did go grocery shopping and, well before Jeff got home from school, they made love. Jeff finally came rolling in at about 3:30 PM. He immediately ran in and gave his dad a hug. After that the questions were nonstop. Jeff wanted to know exactly how much Jason had won but Jason was elusive in his answer. He did say, however, that he would now be okay without a job for a while. While he was thinking about it, he called his headhunter and asked him if had found any new leads. The headhunter said that there seemed to nothing in Denver and that perhaps he should think about relocating. Jason then asked him if he had heard anything about Arizona. John, the headhunter, replied that the Phoenix area was supposedly booming. This excited Jason as Sandy lived just outside Phoenix in Scottsdale.

A little later they called Jim. Jim was extremely glad to hear from them as he had been considerably worried about his father. He knew only that Jason had lost his job and had taken off to Las Vegas in an attempt win enough money to last until he could find another job. This had upset him as he had assumed that his father intended to cheat. Katy had already assured him that this wasn't the case but Jim wanted to know all the details. When Jason told of the time slips and how he learned to invoke them, Jim was somewhat skeptical about them and Jason could hardly blame him. He simply told him to ask Katy and Jeff and that he would provide proof. He offered to prove it over the phone but Jim said that this would not be necessary. He told Jason that he was indeed going to get his scholarship for his remaining two semesters so he would no longer be a financial burden. Of course room and board still had to be paid for and these weren't cheap. Getting the scholarship back was a matter of pride more than anything else.

That evening Jason broached the subject of relocation to Katy. "There are no jobs her," he said. I talked to my headhunter this morning and he told me than the Denver area is probably one of the worst in the country as far as jobs in software engineering. What do you think about moving?"

"Well I suppose there's nothing holding us here," said Katy. "Our parents have passed on and our brothers and sisters are spread all over the country. Do you have any idea where we might go."

"Yes I do," answered Jason. I told you about the friend I made in Vegas—Sandy. Well, Sandy happens to live in Scottsdale, Arizona and he told me that they're hiring programmers in his area. I asked our headhunter the same question and he said that Phoneix is a hot area. I think we ought to sell our house and move there."

Katy seemed to approve of the idea so they decided to sleep on it and then talk to Jeff to see how he felt about it. Jeff had just broken with his "true love" so they didn't expect that he would have many objections. If they were all in agreement they would call Jim.

Chapter 13

Jason woke up at 5 AM and was unable to go back to sleep. He decided that it was time to see what he could learn about the this phenomenon called "time." After getting a cup of coffee he went to his bookshelves and secured the two books he had that might provide him with some information. One was by the acclaimed theoretical physicist, Stephen Hawking. Jason had little hope of discovering anything that might help him but he thought that he should at least acquaint himself with the subject of time.

The first thing he learned was that the concept of time has no meaning before the beginning of the universe. He was not sure that this made any sense. Didn't time just roll on no matter what was around? St Augustine said that time was a property of the universe that God created and it did not exist before the beginning of the universe. This didn't make much sense either but Jason had to accept it despite his doubts.

Both Aristotle and Newton believed in absolute time. This meant that that one could measure the interval of time between two events and that the measurement would be the same regardless of who measured it (as long as everyone had reliable clocks). This made perfect sense to Jason and he supposed that he must classify himself as an absolutist.

Jason then got into some complicated stuff which concluded with the statement that Einstein's theory of relativity put an end to the idea of absolute time. Also one must accept the fact that time is not completely from and independent of space, but is combined with it to form an object called space time. In a way time could be thought as a fourth coordinate.

Next came some interesting material. Time appears to run slower near a massive body like the earth. To someone high up it would appear that everything below was taking longer to happen. This prediction was tested in 1962, using a pair of very accurate clocks mounted at the top and bottom of a water tower. The clock at the bottom, which was nearer the earth was found to run slower, in exact agreement with general relativity. The difference in the speed of clocks can very critical in accurate navigation systems that are based on signals from satellites.

Now Jason read about the apparently famous twins' paradox. If one twin goes to live on the top of a mountain while the other stays at sea level, the latter one would age faster. The difference would be small but would be much greater if the one on the mountain were to go for a long trip in a spaceship going the speed of light.

The twin's paradox was indeed fascinating but Jason could find nothing with which to compare with his own situation. In the twin's case he would take the position of the twin on the ground but what implications would that have?—only that time would run faster for him than it would for someone living high in the mountains.

There was also a lot of talk about the speed of light but Jason wasn't sure how to fit this into the equation. What did the frequency of light have to do with time? As light goes up in a gravitational field it loses energy and its frequency goes down. This means that the length of time between one wave crest and the next goes up. Thus time is slowing down. To an observer it would appear that everything below was taking longer to happen.

At this juncture Jason opened his second book. He had little hope—expecting just a rehash of what he had already covered. The section of the book that dealt with time did indeed begin with the assertion that before the creation of the universe there was no time. After that the book got into such involuted complexities that Jason gave up.

By this time Jason was getting hungry and decided to go to the kitchen and fry up some bacon and eggs as Katy would be getting up shortly to prepare for work. He got the eggs out of the refrigerator but was unable to find any bacon. He knew there was bacon in the freezer in the garage so he went to the door that led to the garage. He opened the door just in time to hear a loud band and felt a sharp pain in his chest. As he fell he attempted to concentrate on the initials NISS and suddenly he was back at the kitchen refrigerator. He realized then what had happened. Someone had broken into the garage and when he opened the door whoever the burglar was had shot him. He realized that he could simply just not open the door and the burglar might leave rather than attempt to break in. Then he realized that this wasn't enough and was not fair to his neighbors who might well become the intruder's next victims He had to get the man off the street. He then unlocked the door that led to the garage but didn't open it. He positioned himself to the side of the door. In a matter of 10 seconds or so the door opened and a man stepped through holding a pistol. Jason quickly chopped downwards with the edge of his right hand and the pistol fell to the floor. The kitchen was almost dark except for the open refrigerator but Jason was able to see the burglar sufficiently well to land a hard right hand punch to the face followed by a hard left hook to the solar plexus. The burglar bent over at the waist and Jason grabbed him around the neck and brought up his right knee to meet the man's face. He could hear the sickening crack of nose bones and the intruder went down on his back unconscious.

Katy entered the kitchen at that moment and let out a cry of alarm. "It's all right," reassured Jason. "He's unconscious. He broke into the garage and shot me when I was going out to get some bacon. I did a time slip and took care of everything the second time. Call the police while I keep an eye on this guy."

Katy complied just as the burglar was regaining consciousness with a groan as he felt the pain of his ruined face. Jason covered the man with his own gun and told him not to try anything as he would love to end the man's criminal career. Wisely the burglar complied. Jeff then entered the room, having been awakened by the sounds of the struggle although the gunshot had now never occurred. Within 5 minutes a patrol car arrived at the Bricker's with siren screaming.

The police questioned Jason and were satisfied with his explanation but were amazed that Jason had been able to disarm the man so easily." I learned a few things in Vietnam," Jason explained.

Chapter 14

After their little adventure Katy continued with breakfast. "I've been doing some study to try and figure out how time works," said Jason," but all I'm doing is getting more confused."

As they began eating Jason told Katy about the paradox of the twins and the water tower consideration. "I just don't see how any of this applies to me," said Jason. "And I still don't understand what the frequency of light has to do with time."

"Well, let's just face it dear," said Katy. "You're weird. By the way what are you two going to do today."

"Oh, I forgot that Jeff's out for the summer," said Jason. "For one thing I'll get some new tires on the BMW. We're been putting that off for 6 months. Then if he feels like it maybe we'll play golf."

Jeff got up shortly thereafter and they said good bye to Katy for the day. "Have fun," she said, "and don't let dad cheat at golf. I'm sure he can figure some way to do it with his super powers."

Upon inspecting Jeff's car, a 2003 Infiniti G3, he decided that the car also needed new rubbers. They took care of this chore and bought top of the line Michelins for both cars. Jim would be next when he brought his 2003 Acura SUV into town.

Once they had the automobiles had taken care of they took Jeff's car home, loaded up their golf clubs, and headed for a local course that they frequented. The course had formerly been a country club and was quite difficult. Straight shots were required and Jason was a big swinger without a lot of accuracy. Since it was now the middle of the day they didn't anticipate the course being very crowded.

"Do you like your clubs?" Jason asked his son.

"Yeah, they're fine," answered Jeff not realizing that his father was really asking him if he wanted new clubs. Jason himself was also well satisfied. He had purchased a used set of King Cobra irons several years previously and found them very forgiving. He also had an oversized driver with which he was sometimes able to hit the ball over 300 yards.

He had two small Titliest metal fairway woods with which he was occasionally able to hit some very good shots. These however weren't very forgiving and Jason had decided to sell them on EBAY and buy some with larger heads. One advantage of the metal woods was that their small heads could cut through long grass whereas an oversized head would get hung up to some extent.

"Mine are too," said Jason. "At least for now."

It didn't take Jason long to figure out how to use a time slip to his advantage while golfing. One the third hole he hooked his drive deep into the rough on the right. He concentrated on NISS and found himself about to take his driver from the bag. This time he chose a 3 wood and, with a short compact swing, drove the ball straight down the middle of the fairway. Jeff had no idea of what happened but Jason admitted to cheating.

"That's cool, Dad, "he exclaimed. Can you keep hitting the same shot over and over again?"

Strangely this was something that Jason had forgotten Of course it was possible to do multiple time slips over the same period. "Let's find out next hole," he said.

The hole was a tough 178 par 3 over water. Jason selected a 5 iron and proceeded to hit a ball right in the middle of the lake. Jeff laughed uproariously and Jason was soon replaying the shot. He was indeed giving the phrase, "instant replay" new meaning. This time he did better but was still off the green. Again he forced a time slip. After 5 tries he hit a ball 5 fee from the cup.

Jason looked at Jeff, who said, "I guess you don't need to do those time slips if you can hit shots like that on your first try."

Jason then explained that he was actually laying about 15 with all of the penalty strokes involved. Four of my shots went in the lake and you laughed your ass off every time."

"Well, are those balls still in the lake?" asked Jeff, obviously still not understanding the whole matter.

"No," said Jason, "the only ball I've played is the one that's now on the green in shape for a birdie. "You could be a golf pro, dad," said Jeff. "All you need to go is keep hitting a shot till you get it right."

"I think I did enough cheating in Vegas," replied Jason. "From now on it's just one shot—no matter where it goes. As they were playing Jason thought it might be a good time to sound out Jeff regarding

Arizona. "Jeff," he said. "there's something we need to talk about. There's just no jobs for me here so we might have to move to someplace where I can get work."

"But dad," remonstrated Jeff. "You don't really have to work unless you want to. If nothing else you can always just make a run to Vegas. You could always fly too."

"No, I want to make an honest living," said Jason. "I don't understand these time slips and I have no idea how long they'll be around. As long as they are I just want to use them when they are absolutely needed—although it's hard to keep from playing around with them."

"Boy, would I ever do some serious playing around if I were in your shoes!" exclaimed Jeff.

"Anyway, as I was saying, I think we need to move someplace where I can get a job," explained Jason. How would you feel about that."

"I'm not stuck here," answered Jeff. "I've got some friends but nobody that I'm really close to. My high school sucks. I should be on both the football and basketball teams but the coaches seem to have something against me. Yeah, I'm ready to get away. Where are we thinking of going?"

"Well, I understand that there's a lot of jobs in the Phoenix area. One problem is that it's really hot there."

"I can put up with that," said Jeff. "I can't stand the winters here. Hey, can we have a swimming pool?"

"I think we'll have a hard time finding a house that doesn't already have one," answered Jason.

Chapter 15

I t was now 6 PM. Jason and Jeff had been home for about an hour and Katy would be arriving shortly. Jason had just called Jim and talked to him for about 15 minutes. Like Jeff, Jim had no qualms about moving. It was strange but no one in the family seemed to be particularly fond of Denver. Jason had been born in southern Califonia and Katy in Minneapolis. They had met on the UCLA campus as they both played on the basketball teams. It was only NISS that had held them in Denver—held them prisoner in fact. Jim would be arriving home in 3 days for summer break and could thus assist in the move—although Jason intended to also hire a crew of movers who would do the majority of the work. Afterall they could afford it. The first thing they had to do was sell the house and Jason was not about to hold out for the last penny. He would accept any reasonable offer and he had already informed their realtor of that fact.

Once Jim was home the four of them would take a trip to Scottsdale and see what they could find as far as housing. Jason had already called Sandy and told him of their plan. Sandy was, of course, delighted and promised to line them up with a good real estate agent.

Within four days things were moving. Jason and Katy had agreed to an offer on their home—more than Jason would have settled for. Settlement would occur as soon as they moved out. The four of them had caught a flight to Phoneix and Sandy met them at the airport. On the drive to Scottsdale Jason sat in the back seat with the boys. Sandy had a beautiful home to which he took them and insisted that they stay there while in Scottsdale as he plenty of room. Both of his children were attending summer sessions at the University of Mexico in Albuquerque. Jason was already aware of this but Sandy spoke for the benefit of Katy, Jim and Jeff. The boys both liked Sandy because he treated them as adults. Sandy explained to them that he had lost his first house in the divorce but was able to afford his current home after winning a few big legal cases.

Sandy suggested that they take a swim in his pool after they arrived at his house and they were happy to oblige. As they were swimming Sandy brought out a large vodka collins for Jason. Katy wasn't normally much of a drinker but on this occasion she opted for a vodka gimlet which Sandy handily prepared. Jim had a beer and Jeff a coke. While they were poolside Sandy called the real estate agent with whom he had been dealing and an appointment was set up for the next day. Jason lay in the sun and wondered if he didn't have the cart before the horse. They had indeed sold their home but he didn't yet have a job. Oh well, he thought. Things will work out. He did have his best suit with him, a suit he had purchased from a genuine tailor—the first Jason had ever consulted. His 6' 2" inches of height and 195 pound muscular body were displayed to his advantage. The time in Vegas had been the longest span of his adult life during which he failed to lift weights or jog. Actually Jason had done a series of push-ups and sit-ups each morning in Vegas and walked for miles in getting from one casino to another. He had also done some jogging on several occasions.

Once he had the job there would be no reason to prolong closing on a house and Jason hoped to have that taken care of after his first interview the following day. He realized that he was being overly optimistic but everything worked out as planned. Jason's interview was with IBM and they hired him immediately for 100K per year. Katy had also found a job at the Veteran's hospital in Scottsdale. Jeff's high school could wait until they had made the move. After three short days the four of them took a plane back to Denver to supervise the move.

Chapter 16

I t was just a matter of days before Jason and his family were ready to make the trip back to Scottsdale. The moving van had already pulled out and they were left with 4 automobiles—vehicles that had to be driven 810 miles. They didn't intend to make the drive in one day—they would overnight in Flagstaff and had already reserved two rooms at a Comfort Inn because they all liked the motel chain. Gasing up the 4 cars was a matter of almost $200 but Jason had plenty of money. He and Katy had kept two credit cards for the purpose of motels, etc. They also retained a prepaid Visa for Internet use. Jason was determined that no one was to get tired—if someone had to stop and rest they would all stop. He was the only one who had control of time and it had been sheer luck that one of his time slips had saved him on the drive from Las Vegas to Denver. They had four cell phones so that they could communicate while driving. None of them liked to use the phone unless they were stopped but would make an exception on this drive.

The drive went without incident—not even a flat tire. They halted in Albuquerque for dinner at about 4 PM and decided to spend the night there and call and cancel their reservation in Flagstaff . . . They stayed at a Roadside Inn after first checking out the rooms at their own insistence. Jason and Jim had their own room while Jason and Katy stayed in another.

The next day's driving was relatively short and they arrived in Scottsdale at about 1 PM. The moving van was already there and Sandy was supervising the unloading of furniture. Katy had already given him an idea of where to have the furniture placed but, as women were wont to do, she had now changed her mind. They were just in time to make a change as to where to put the piano. All four of them were determined to learn to play the piano but no one had taken lessons. They could all play Yankee Doodle and that was about it although Jason had memorized one of Beethoven's sonatas. Katy now took charge of the remaining furniture and beds. They called Sandy and he stopped by. Jason then asked for directions about how to keep the swimming pool clean. "If you don't get some expert help you'll have a swamp that's only fit for piranhas and alligator," stated Sandy.

By about 4 PM the house was pretty much in order. Of course there remained a myriad of small tasks that would take weeks to accomplish. They then went shopping at a local Target which Sandy also frequented and had told them about. After putting the groceries away Jason and Katy decided to take a walk through their subdivision. They soon decided that they were very pleased with their location. They decided to keep on walking until they reached a major road. Suddenly a girl shot by them on a bicycle and into the street. She had no chance as she pedaled directly into the path of an oncoming pickup. The truck driver hit his brakes but it was far too late. The impact was horrendous and both the bicycle and the girl were sent flying through the air. Immediately Jason attempted to invoke a time slip and was successful. He could see the broken and bloody body of the girl lying some 20 yard down the street. The time slip then kicked in and Katy's scream was suddenly stifled. The girl was approaching on her bicycle and Jason grabbed the handlebars and brought the bike to a stop. The girl cried out something about letting her go but now Jason was angry. For one thing the front tire of the bicycle had impacted him in the crotch. "Your parents should take that bike away if you're going to ride it like that!" exclaimed Jason. Well I'll tell you what. Get off that bike, wait for the light and then walk it across the street in the crosswalk."

Katy was looking perplexed. "What just happened, Jason. It's got something to do with those time lapses of yours. I know you just don't grab little girls and treat them like that," she continued.

"Katy, that little girl was just killed. I saw the whole thing. You saw how fast she was riding. There was no way she was going to stop for the light. She didn't and that pickup that just went by past hit her. It knocked both her and bike for 60 or 70 feet."

"My God, you saved her life!," exclaimed Katy.

"Yes and I almost spanked her," retorted Jason.

"Well she needs to spanked," continued Katy. "The only problem is that we can't do it without getting into all kinds of trouble. We should have tried to find out where she lives and now she's out of sight. Her parents need to be told."

"The problem is that they can't see what I saw. If they could they'd probably take her bike away and it would suit her right."

That night Jason and his family went out with Sandy. He had a date for the evening, a beautiful blond girl named Bonnie who seemed very friendly. His children, Megan and Thomas were also home for the weekend and seemed to be getting along famously with Jim and Jeff. Jeff, as usual, was the life of the party and kept everyone in stitches with his dry sense of humor. When Jason got a chance he told Sandy about the girl and the bicycle.

"You obviously did the right thing," said Sandy. "I just wish you didn't have to use that power. Sooner or later it's going to get you into trouble."

Jason agreed but remained silent.

Chapter 17

The next few days were spent getting the house in living shape. There was indeed much to be done. When the appropriate offices were opened Jason arranged for electrical and natural gas service. He also called a swimming pool cleaning company, having decided not to try to maintain the pool himself. He arranged for someone to come out to service and inspect the central air unit—an indispensable appliance for any southern Arizona home. Swamp coolers were also popular in Arizona so Jason planned to evaluate their power bills and make a change if advisable. Next he contacted Comcast to arrange for the same bundled services they had enjoyed in Denver—cable TV, high-speed Internet and landline phone service. He was pleased that he was able to get this service for $177.99 per month. He didn't think he would have to make any changes to their Verizon cell phone plan but called them just in case. He also arranged for sewer and water. These chores took up most of the morning.

While Jason was doing his bit towards organization the rest of the family had been doing their part. They were turning a house into a home and doing a good job of it. They were beginning to feel that they belonged. At about noon there was a knock at the door. Jeff answered and greeted Sandy. "Whassup, Mr. Nelson?"

"I've got a little news," said Sandy said after an exchange of greetings." Bonnie and I are getting married next week."

The rest of the family congratulated Sandy and Katy gave him a sound kiss on the cheek. He shook hands with the male members of the family and informed that he and Bonnie had been dating regularly for three months and thing were definitely clicking.

"By the way," he said, "we want to go water skiing at Lake Pleasant this afternoon and we wondered if you wanted to go. You've been working hard and you deserve it. Aside from that we can't ski anyway unless there is someone else in the boat to serve as a 'watcher. We don't know if my kids are going yet or not. If they do my boat will be a little crowed but we'll make do. It's a 20 footer with 6 seats so we should be fine. Two people will be skiing most of the time anyway."

Jason readily agreed to go after consulting with Katy and the boys. Jason was a little concerned as he had skied only once in his life. Jeff and Jim had done considerable skiing with their friends in Denver. Jeff told Jason not to worry as it was actually quite easy. Jason knew better, as he had always had a hard time in taking up a new sport, etc. "About this boating thing," he said. "I didn't think they had enough water for a boat in Arizona.

We've got all kinds of lakes here," said Sandy "and I'll have you know that Arizona leads the nation in boats per-capita. Not many people know that but it's true."

Jason told them that he only tried water skiing one time and that had been 25 years previously. He also mentioned that the longest he was ever able to stay upright was about 5 seconds. As soon as he was forced to go over a wake he was lost.

"We'll fix that," advised Sandy.

The drive to Lake Pleasant took a little over an hour and was quite scenic. Sandy did indeed have a nice boat but it was a little overcrowded once they all got in. "Don't worry about the crowding," said Sandy." We're going to have two skiers in the water for most of the time."

Megan and Thomas went first and they were both excellent skiers. Next came Jeff and Jim. Jim was a good skier but Jeff was a prodigy. He had skied often in Denver and entertained everyone with all sorts of tricks. They all thought he would fall but he never did.

"Well, it's your turn," said Sandy, looking at Jason.

"You'd better let me go alone," said Jason, "because I'll fall about every 10 feet."

A minute later Jason was in the water and the skis were on. He dropped his upraised right hand as a go signal and Sandy accelerated the boat. Jason climbed from the water and did fine for about 5 seconds before he had to cross a wake. Then a ski dipped into a wave and he was airborne, landing on his chest and forgetting to let go of the tow rope. His skis came off and the boat was pulling him farther underwater until he remembered that he was still holding the rope.

"Keep you weight back on your skis," instructed Sandy "and you'll be fine"

Jason tried again but wiped out again although he did make it for about 10 seconds.

"One more try," he yelled. This time when he fell Jason invoked a time slip. When he again had to cross a wake he leaned back on his skis and watched them go over the wake. It was almost as if he jumped but lost his balance upon landing, regained control and continued to ski. After several more attempts he thought he had the skiing down and now concentrated on keeping his balance and "lookin' good." Once he was on board the boat Sandy congratulated him.

"Sandy," said Jason. I fell down about 20 times before I finally caught on. I just covered up the falls with time slips.

"Whatever works," replied his friend.

Katy and Bonnie next skied together. Both were very adept. Katy had skied a lot as a child as her father had owned a boat. Also the two were rapidly becoming friends. Bonnie wanted to know all about Jason's "ailment" and Katy was willing to discuss the matter and get an objective opinion.

The afternoon was very enjoyable and the two families were closer together than ever. It was obvious to Jason that his friendship for Sandy had blossomed into more of a family friendship.

Chapter 18

The next day Jason reported for work for the first time. He could have taken a few more days off but he was anxious to get started. The first thing he had to do was to fill out some paperwork and have his picture taken for a badge. Next he was shown to his desk and introduced to his new manager. Tim seemed to be a friendly unassuming person and Jason felt immediately that he could work for him. They talked a little about general plant procedure and rules, none of which were surprises for Jason. Next they began discussion of Tim's group's current project. The coding was to be done in Visual Basic, a language that Jason had just learned and barely began to use at NISS. The project appealed to him and he was anxious to get started.

At 12:00 PM Tim stopped by Jason's cubicle and asked if he would like to go to lunch in the cafeteria. "For a cafeteria the food's not that bad," promised Tim. As they ate Tim and Jason talked constantly. It turned out that they had a great deal in common—including a love for Texas Hold'em and other poker games. Jason had to laugh to himself as Tim began talking about quarter tables. He himself had played on $10,000 tables. Well, now he was back to nickel-dime poker but that was just fine. Eventually he might have to go back to Las Vegas to refuel but the family was fine for the time being. Las Vegas was also somewhat closer although not a great deal. Katy was also to begin work at the VA hospital the next day. After lunch Jason began to write code—the flow charts were already complete and the job was not all that difficult. Quitting time came around but Jason continued to code as this his custom. As he drove home, which was only two miles away, he looked forward to a dip in the pool. His workplace was air conditioned but the air in his car was not working and would have to be taken care of. By the time he reached home he was almost drenched in sweat. When he arrived the boys were already in the pool so Jason joined them. About a half hour later Katy arrived home and they made it a family affair.

After a relaxing and cooling swim Jason barbequed some steaks and they had a nice dinner with homemade French fries and a tossed salad. Then all went their separate ways. Jason had his own Visual Basic compiler which he had purchased for his last project at NISS. Most of the programmers simply took their compiler home which was not actually legal.

After dinner Katy went to her sewing class and Jason went bowling for his new company. The local branch of his IBM company had several teams in a league and Tim had asked him if he bowled. After their steak dinner Jason had located his bowling balls which he had seldom found time to use in Denver. He had purchased two Hammer balls, one of which was a spare ball not to be confused with "extra." The second ball was for use in picking up spares as it tended to hook less than the main ball. Jason had a special tape which was to be applied to the thumbholes of the balls in order to achieve a better fit. Jim had a movie date that night with a girl he had literally run into at Target. He was taking the girl to a movie in downtown Phoenix.

At about 11:00 PM the phone rang and a police officer informed Jason that Jim had been in an automobile accident. Fortunately Jim was the only one in the family who had procured a new driver's license and the police were thus able to track him down and get a phone number. A drunken driver had run a red light and collided with Jim's Acura, totaling the car. The driver of the vehicle was now in the county jail. Jim was being kept in ICU until the exact extent of his injuries could be determined. He definitely had a concussion as well as a broken leg. An Xray of his skull would determine the actual extent of his head injuries but he was conscious. His date had sustained only cuts and bruises and for this Jason and Katy were thankful. Before they left home for the hospital they knelt in prayer asking that Jim would heal rapidly and that no further injuries would be found. Jason spoke the prayer aloud—he believed that a prayer should be essentially a conversation with God and Katy agreed with this philosophy. This was a part of what they liked in each other.

Upon arriving at the hospital they found that Jim had been moved to a private room and was currently sleeping. They decided to wait for a while and see if he awakened. While they were waiting Jason called Jim's health insurance provider and reported the accident. Finally a doctor came out and spoke to them. He told them that Jim was graded now as serious—much better than the critical status he had initially earned.

Jason, Katy and Jeff were in the hospital every day for the week that Jim had to remain there. They enjoyed the opportunity to discuss things with Jim alone. The Jim with whom they were conversing little resembled the bright eyed but naïve youngster that they had sent to Rochester 3 years previously. He was now a very intelligent but inquisitive young man. He wanted to know every detail about Jason's time traveling and had question after question. He speculated that perhaps Jason was just privy to a natural phenomenon—that time in and of itself was rolling back every 60 seconds and that only Jason was aware of this and could utilize it in some way. At the same time he admitted that he knew nothing more about time than did Jason. "It doesn't matter anyway," he concluded. "This far transcends anything that anyone, living or dead, mankind knows about time anyway."

"Well, so am I going back in time or what," queried Jason.

"Based on what you've told me I don't think so," answered Jim—"I think it's time that's going back on you. Time is continually rolling back on you. By the way I want to see your little trick—the one you showed mom and Jeff—" the one where they write something on a piece of paper and then you tell them what they wrote. Some magician would probably pay you a bundle for that trick and then not be able to perform it. Jason obliged and they both had a good laugh as Jim had also written "NISS sucks." I didn't need the time slip for that," Jason chuckled.

"Dad we've got to try and find out more about this. There must be researchers somewhere who can help us. I'm sure there's a government agency that deals with things like this. Also the whole thing could change complexion and we have no idea of where you'd be."

"I agree that I'd like to get some help figuring out what's going on. At the same time I've got a job and don't want to be spending a lot of time as a guinea pig," said Jason

"You still have your freedom dad, and no one can force you to anything you don't want to do. We'll be around to make sure they don't try to infringe on you rights," returned Jim.

Jason took real comfort from Jim's analysis and pride in the fine young man he had become.

In a week Jim was home but in a wheelchair. He was fine except for missing the swimming pool—a fact about which he complained and for which he earned the sobriquet, "pain in the ass," from Jeff.

Chapter 19

On a Saturday morning Jason and Katy rode into Phoenix. Ostensibly they were shopping for Jeff's 18th birthday. They could, however, have managed this adequately in Scottsdale which had everything they might need. Scottsdale was, in fact, its own city and a good-sized one at that. In terms of square miles it ranked second in the state—behind Phoenix. As for population it ranked 5th with 235,000 inhabitants. Thus there was no real reason to go to Phoenix at all except that Jason and Katy wanted to see the city. They picked perhaps a bad day as the U.S. president was to be in town. Streets were blocked everywhere and this made it impossible to get around. Jason and Katy finally decided to see the president and then retreat to Scottsdale for their shopping.

Dan Maclean was indeed a popular man as was attested by sections and sections of bleachers on Main street. Everyone apparently wanted to see the president. A podium was erected on one side of the street where Mclean was to deliver a speech. Jason and Katy paid 5 dollars to park and then walked for a half mile. There were two seats available on the second row of bleachers directly across the street from the podium. Someone was in the process of leaving and offered the seats to Katy who was ahead of Jason. "You don't look a gift horse in the mouth," said Katy as they took their seats. "I can't believe how many people are here," said Jason as he hurriedly picked up Katy's purse and sat down.

"Well it's not every day that you get to see the President of the United States," said Katy.

A procession of cars drove by along with countless police cars and motorcycles. Finally all but police vehicles ceased passing and a black open limousine came into view. Secret servicemen, the president's bodyguards, flanked the vehicles and directed searching stares at the onlookers. Then the man himself was visible—smiling and waving both hands in the air. Jason was reminded of JFK and he was sure that Kathy had the same feeling

Suddenly a shot rang out and the president slumped over in the limousine. It appeared that he had been struck in the head. Jason turned and saw a man holding what appeared to be a plastic toy gun. Immediately Jason concentrated and forced a time slip. As soon as he felt it he took 3 steps to his left and dove over the heads and shoulders of people in the front row. He landed on the dark skinned assassin and sent him sprawling. Two yet unassembled pieces of the plastic gun fell from a blanket the man was carrying.

"Gun here!" someone yelled and a second later Jason and the gunman were surrounded by Secret Service agents. Jason glanced back at Katy and then realized that he was now on the world's stage. If ever he were going to get some understanding of what was happening to him now was the time to start. Every authority or expert would undoubtedly be called in. Already an agent was questioning him as to how he had known that the man had a gun and he answered, "I knew because I saw the man shoot the president before I did a time slip. Now don't ask me any more questions. Sir, could you please grab a piece of paper and write something on it? . . . .